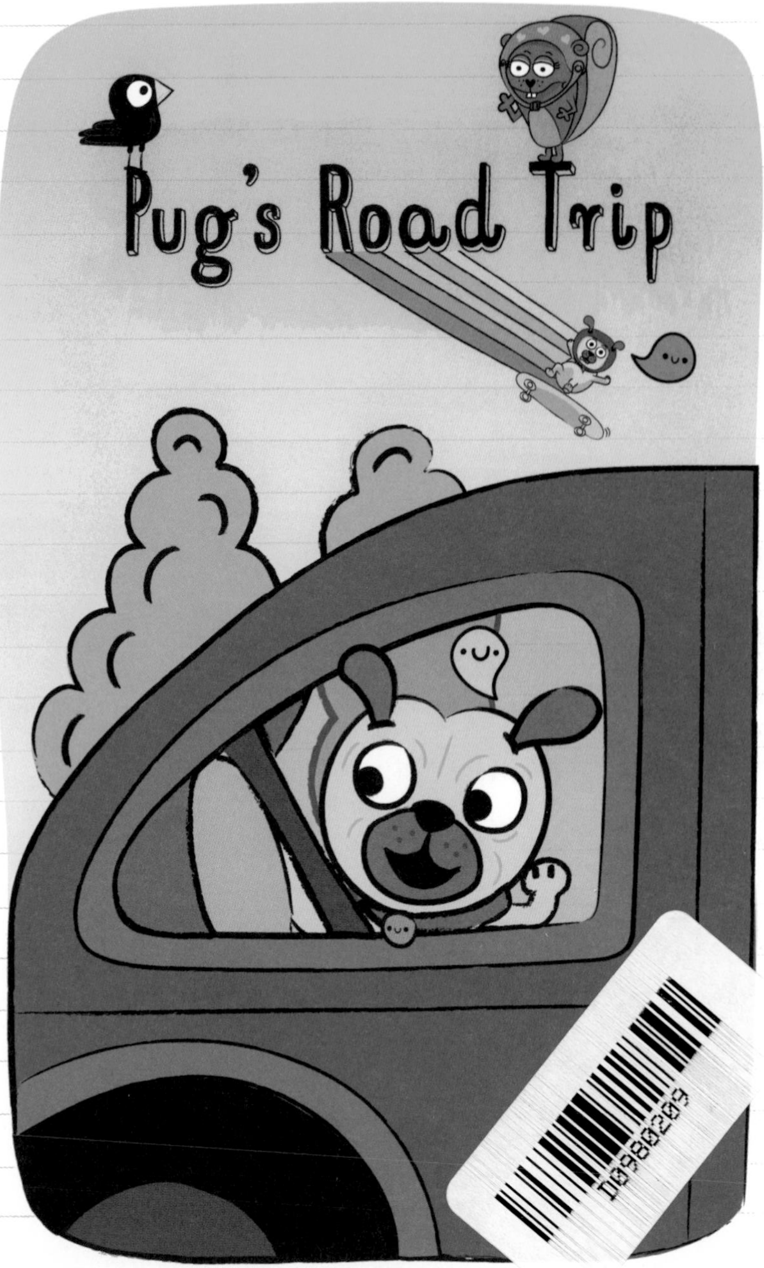
Pug's Road Trip

Read all the Diary of a Pug books!

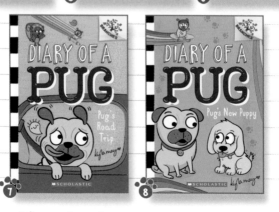

More books coming soon!

DIARY OF A
PUG

Pug's Road Trip

By *Kyla May*

SCHOLASTIC INC.

I dedicate this book to my best friends, who warm my heart and make me laugh always.

Special thanks to Meredith Rusu

Library of Congress Cataloging-in-Publication Data

Names: May, Kyla, author, illustrator. | May, Kyla. Diary of a pug ; 7. Title: Pug's road trip / by Kyla May. Description: First edition. | New York : Branches/Scholastic Inc., 2022. | Series: Diary of a pug ; #7 | Audience: Ages 6–8. | Audience: Grades 2–3. | Summary: When their friend Jack cannot join them, Bub the pug and his human, Bella, vow to bring him souvenirs from their road trip, and despite some bumps along the way, Bub calls their trip a big success. Identifiers: LCCN 2021042984 (print) | ISBN 9781338713503 (paperback) | ISBN 9781338713510 (library binding) Subjects: LCSH: Pug—Juvenile fiction. | Squirrels—Juvenile fiction. | Human–animal relationships—Juvenile fiction. | Voyages and travels—Juvenile fiction. | Theft—Juvenile fiction. | Diaries—Juvenile fiction. | CYAC: Pug—Fiction. | Dogs—Fiction. | Squirrels—Fiction. | Human–animal relationships—Fiction. | Voyages and travels—Fiction. | Diaries—Fiction. | LCGFT: Diary fiction. Classification: LCC PZ7.M4535 Pwh 2022 (print) | LCC PZ7.M4535 (ebook) | DDC [Fic]—dc23 LC record available at https://lccn.loc.gov/2021042984 LC ebook record available at https://lccn.loc.gov/2021042985 978-1-338-71351-0 (reinforced library binding) / 978-1-338-71350-3 (paperback)

10 9 8 7 6 5 4 3 2 1   22 23 24 25 26

Printed in China   62
First edition, October 2022
Edited by Mia Licciardi
Book design by Kyla May and Christian Zelaya

Table of Contents

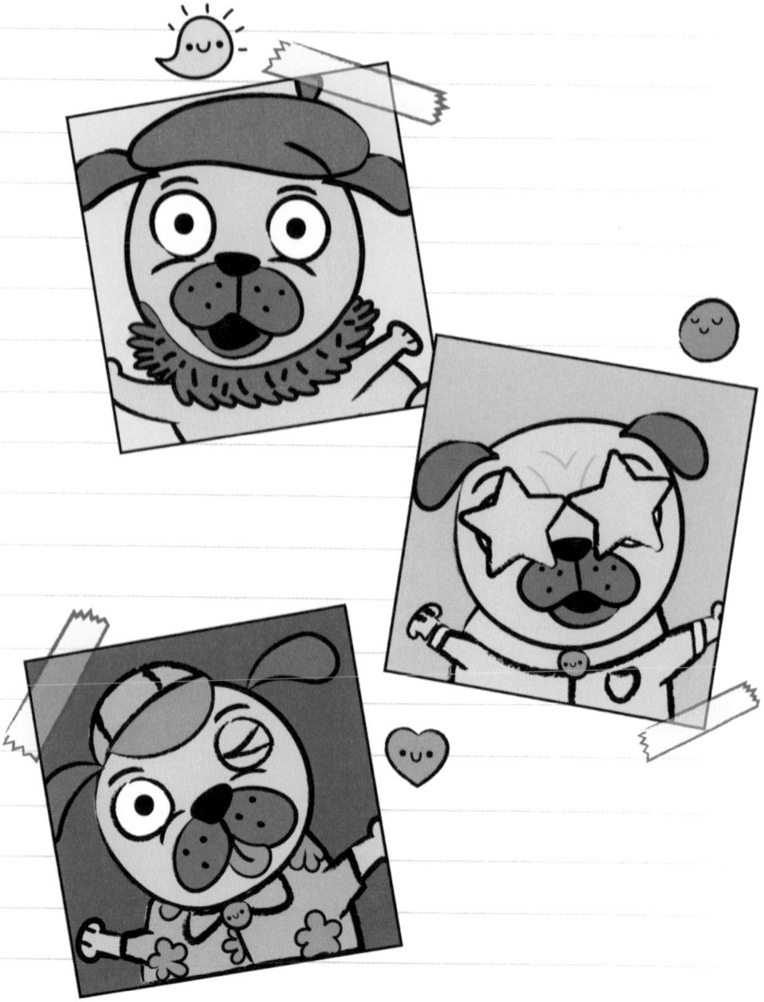

Chapter 1

THE ROAD TO ADVENTURE

SUNDAY

Dear Diary,

Hey there! **BUB** here. But I won't be here for long. Bella says we're hitting the road. Let me tell you about our BIG plans.

But first, here are some things to know about me.

I've got a BIG sense of style.

<u>I make many different faces:</u>

Adventure Face

Chilling Face

Just Sniffed My Butt Face

These are some of my favorite things:

MY SKATEBOARD

PEANUT BUTTER TREATS

RIDING IN THE CAR

Here are some things that get on my nerves:

And, of course, WATER.

Baths, rain, pools, puddles—they're all the worst! It's funny, since water is how I got my full name, BARON VON BUBBLES. I jumped into a bubble bath when Bella first brought me home. I didn't know there was WATER under the bubbles!

BELLA

But anyway, back to our BIG plans.

We're going on a road trip! Mom let me plan the stops.

We're going to see four BIG things. I'm calling it "Bella and Bub's BIG Road Trip!"

I like the sound of that!

Bella said our friends Jack and Luna were coming with us. And we were leaving in the morning.

We had to start packing!

Let's see. I'll need my camera, of course.

Will you help me choose which outfits to bring, Bub?

Let's bring them all!

Diary, did you know you need outfits
for all sorts of activities on a road trip?

DRIVING OUTFIT

HIKING OUTFIT

SWIMMING OUTFIT

Can't forget this!

Wait . . . why are you packing your swimsuit?

I don't know how I'm going to sleep, Diary. What BIG things will we see on our trip? What's Bella's special surprise?

Chapter 2

HITTING THE ROAD

MONDAY

Dear Diary,

We were about to hit the road this morning when the phone rang.

Hey, Jack! Ready to go?

Have fun on your trip, Bubbykins. Don't get lost.

Can that really happen?

Bella and I raced next door.

Jack had a cast on one leg.

Oh, Jack!
What happened?

I fell and broke my leg at camp.
Now I can't go on the road trip.

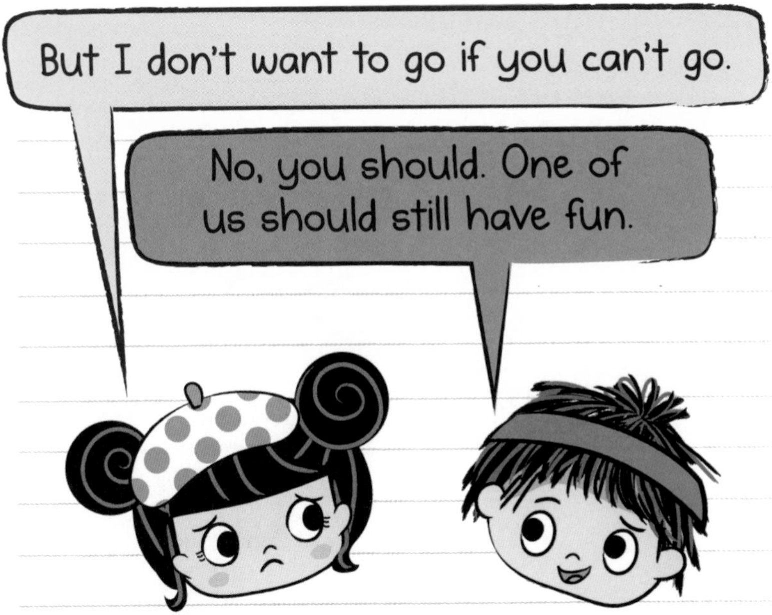
But I don't want to go if you can't go.
No, you should. One of us should still have fun.

I was sad Jack and Luna couldn't come.

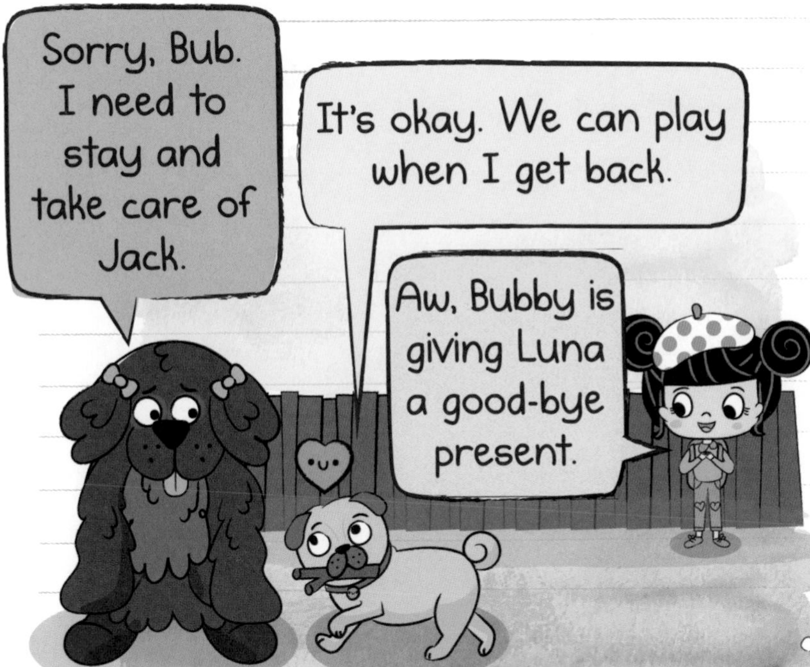
Sorry, Bub. I need to stay and take care of Jack.
It's okay. We can play when I get back.
Aw, Bubby is giving Luna a good-bye present.

Hey, that gives me an idea! We can bring back LOTS of presents for you, Jack—souvenirs from our road trip.

That would be awesome! Thanks!

The trip wouldn't be the same without Jack and Luna. But we would DEFINITELY bring them back lots of cool stuff.

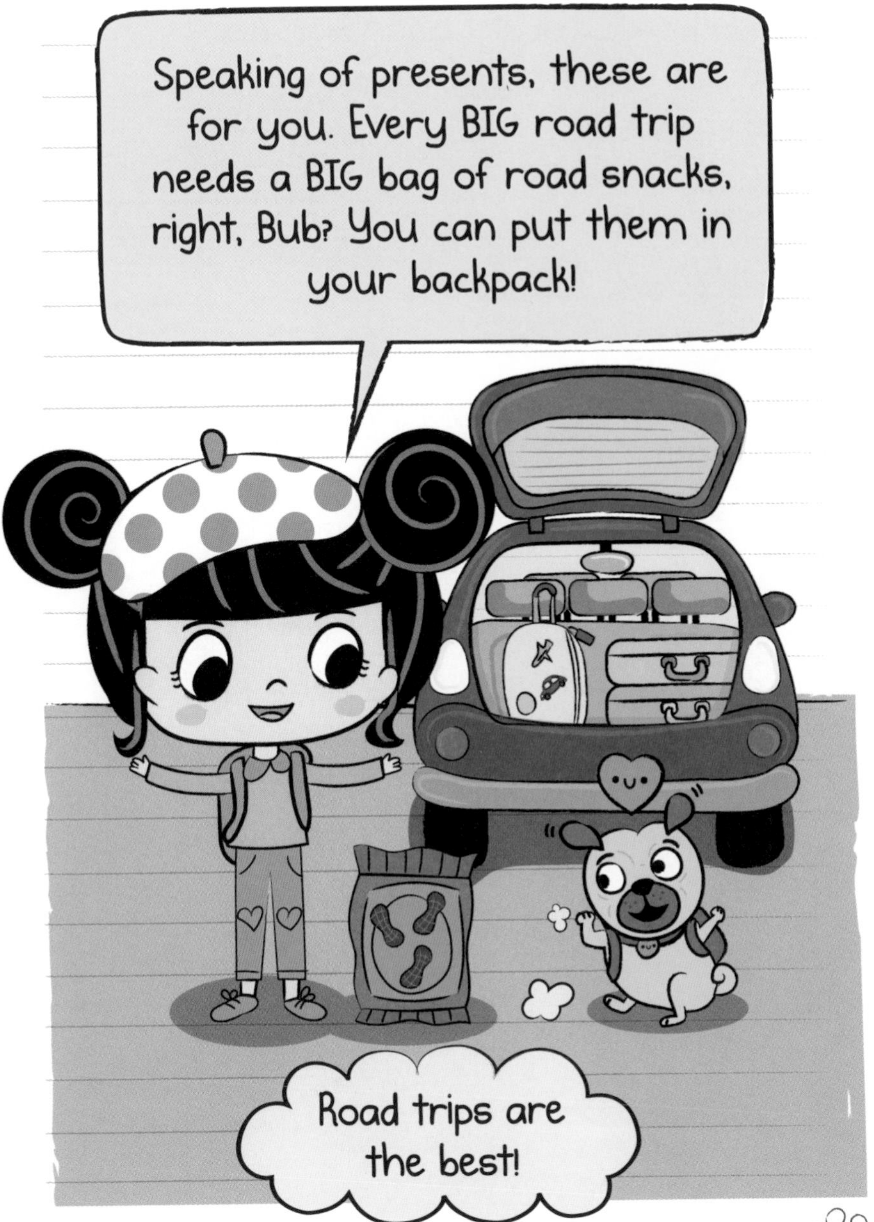
Speaking of presents, these are for you. Every BIG road trip needs a BIG bag of road snacks, right, Bub? You can put them in your backpack!
Road trips are the best!

Suddenly, I heard a familiar noise. One I would definitely NOT miss while we were away.

Sure, sure. Oh, by the way, I let my cousins know that you'd be passing by.

They'll be watching for you.

Wait! What?

That didn't sound good, Diary. But just then, Bella's mom honked the horn. It was time to hit the road!

Bella and Bub's BIG Road Trip

We reached the edge of our town and kept driving.

We reached the edge of our state and kept driving!

We kept driving, and driving, and driving. Guess what, Diary? A big road trip means there's plenty of time for a BIG nap. See you when we get there!

Chapter 3

ROAD TRIP TRICKS

TUESDAY

Dear Diary,

We stayed in a motel last night. They had free breakfast!

We can make our own waffles, Bub!

With peanut butter!

Now we're off to our first BIG stop.

This stop is just for you, Bub!

We're going to the biggest skate park in the country!

This flyer says it's got ramps and half-pipes and something called the Whirlpool.

A whirlpool? That doesn't mean there's water, does it?

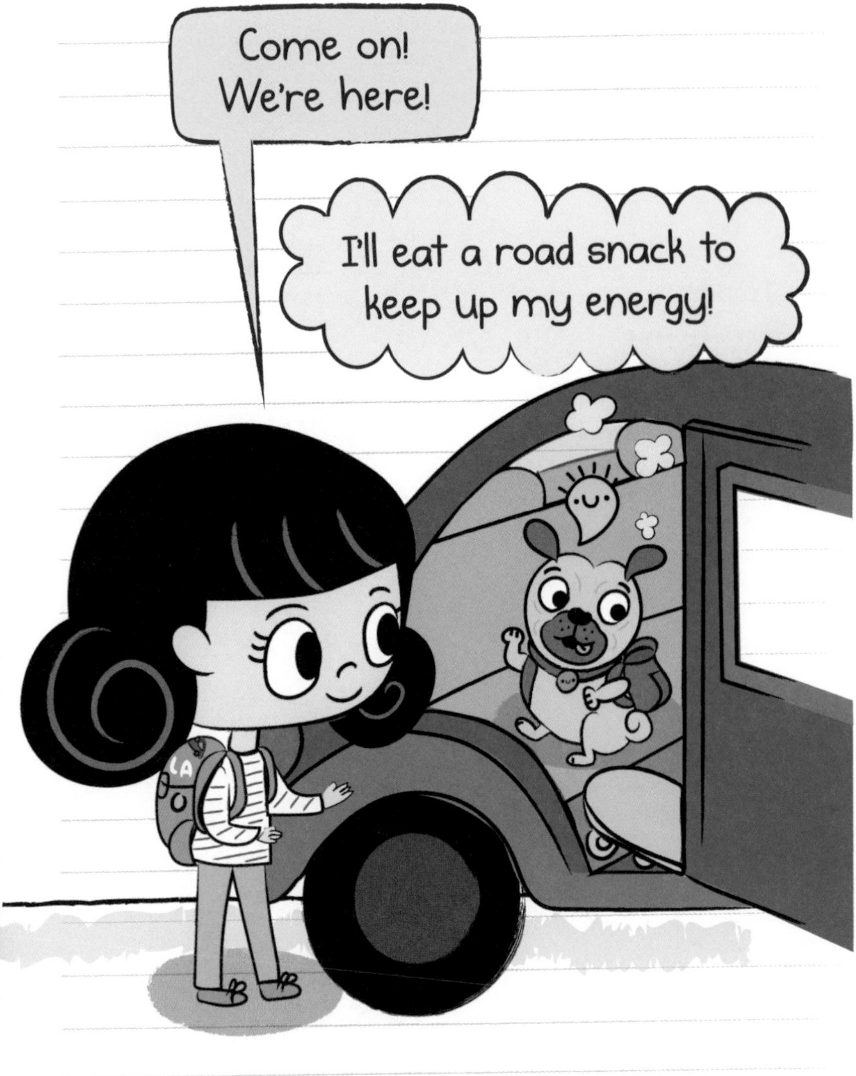
Come on! We're here!
I'll eat a road snack to keep up my energy!

The flyer wasn't kidding, Diary. This place was HUGE.

SKATE SHOP

THE WHIRLPOOL

I spent hours doing front flips and backflips and rail tricks. I even braved the Whirlpool. It had NO water at all, so it was the perfect pool for me!

FRONT FLIP

RAIL TRICK

THE WHIRLPOOL

We stopped by the skate shop, too.

Jack is going to love this key chain!

Do they make this shirt in pug size?

I BRAVED THE WHIRLPOOL

I BRAVED THE WHIRLPOOL

Bella put Jack's souvenir in her backpack. We went back outside. Suddenly, I heard a chitter-chatter sound. It couldn't be . . .

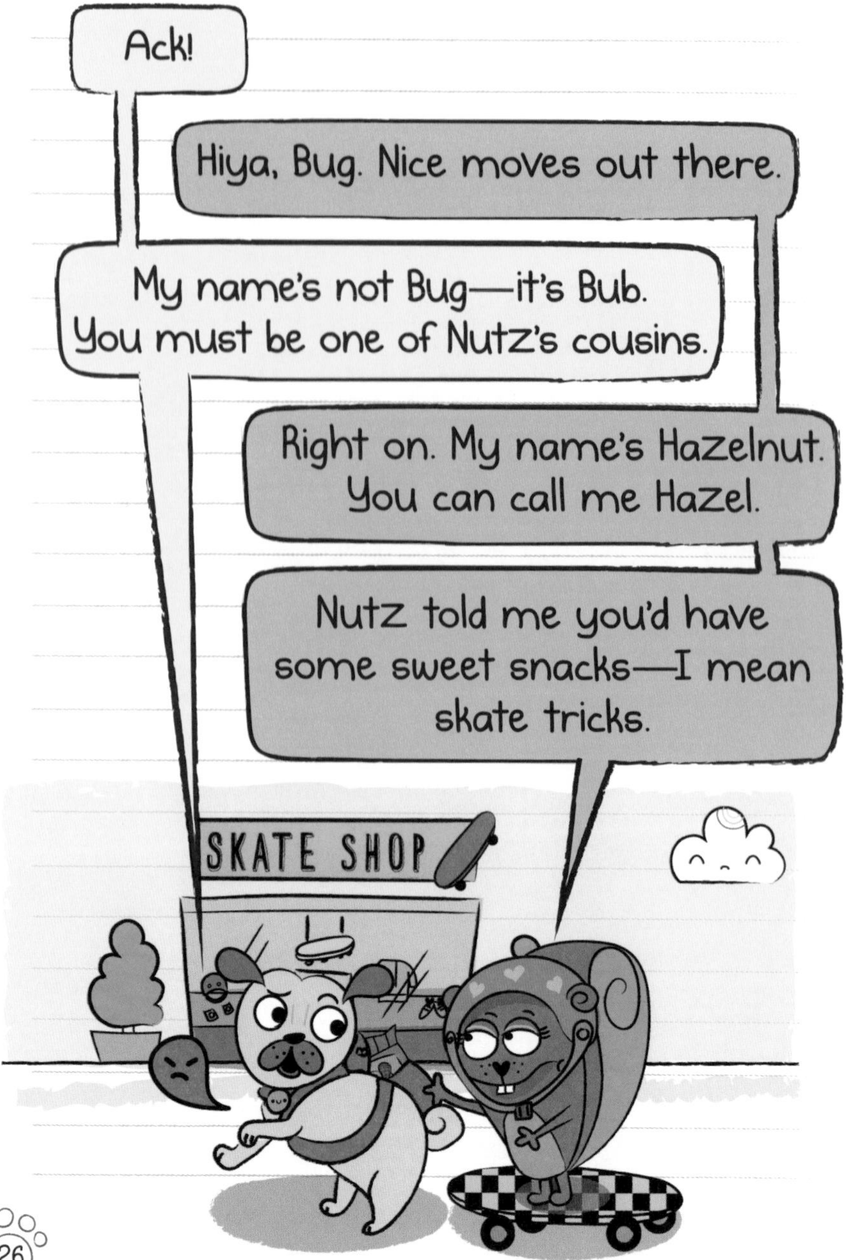
Ack!
Hiya, Bug. Nice moves out there.
My name's not Bug—it's Bub. You must be one of Nutz's cousins.
Right on. My name's Hazelnut. You can call me Hazel.
Nutz told me you'd have some sweet snacks—I mean skate tricks.
SKATE SHOP

Hey! These treats aren't for you!

Relax, Bug. I'm just giving you something.

Nutz said you were into style. When I saw this wheel lying on the ground, I thought, "Bug will love this for his collar."

For my collar? Uh . . . thanks?

That was weird, Diary. I'm used to squirrels taking stuff from me. Not giving me presents. Was Hazel trying to take my snacks? I may never know. But at least the skate park was fun.

I wonder where we're headed to next?

Chapter 4

ROADSIDE BITES

WEDNESDAY

Dear Diary,

This morning, Bella told me to save room for lunch.

Stop two on Bella and Bub's Big Road Trip is the biggest diner in the country!

Diary, I didn't know such a glorious place could exist. I'd left my snacks in the car, but this was just fine.

Welcome to Big Bronco's Diner! Where the only thing bigger than our specials are our peanut butter moon pies.

Look at that, Bub! It's like they were made for you!

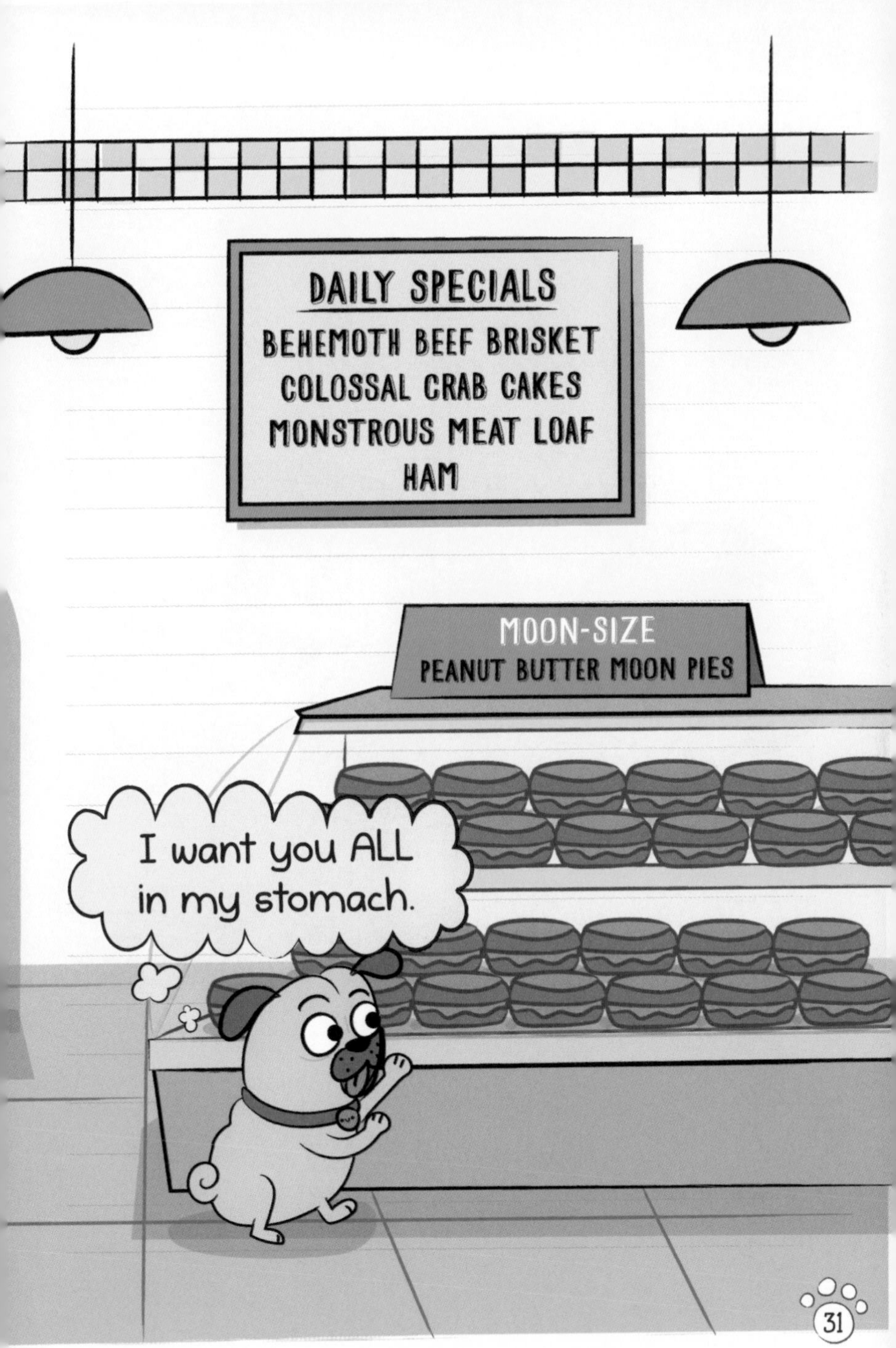
DAILY SPECIALS
BEHEMOTH BEEF BRISKET
COLOSSAL CRAB CAKES
MONSTROUS MEAT LOAF
HAM
MOON-SIZE
PEANUT BUTTER MOON PIES
I want you ALL in my stomach.

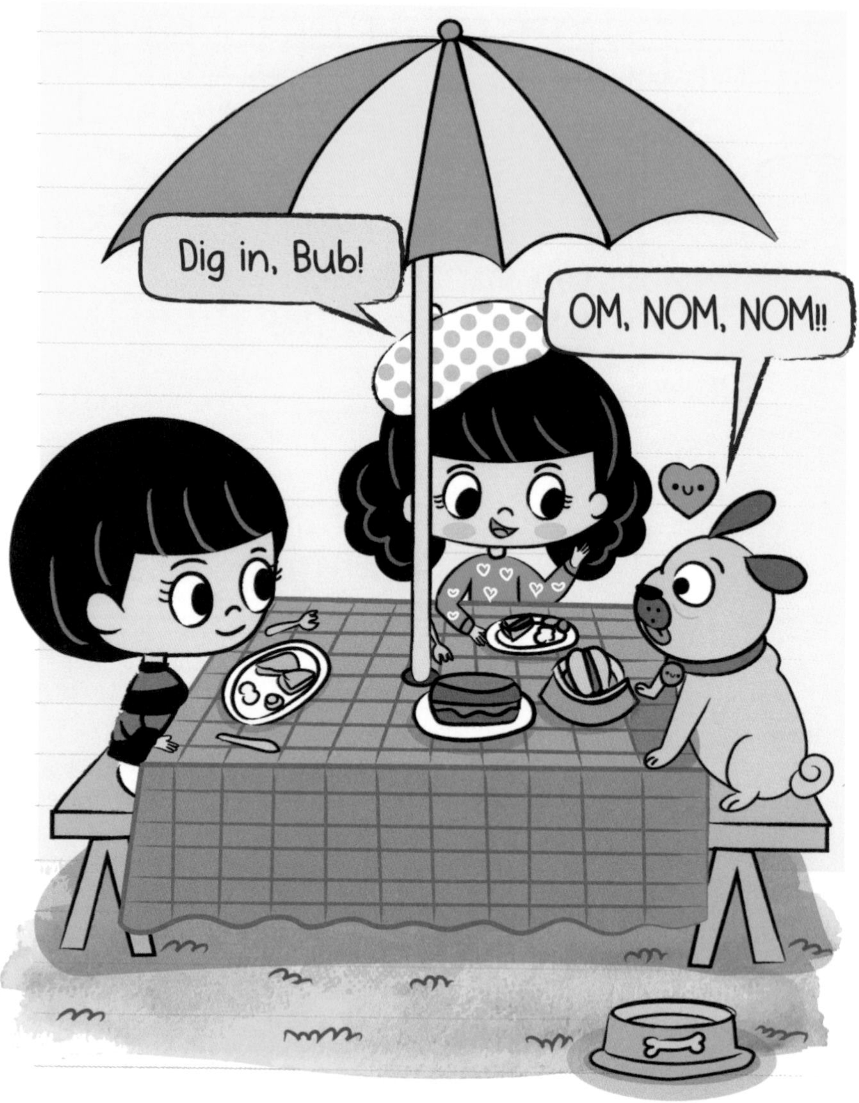
Dig in, Bub!
OM, NOM, NOM!!

The diner even had a shop. Bella picked out just the right gift for Jack.

I bet this is the only place in the world we could get a snow globe with a daily special inside!

HAM

I looked out the store window while Bella paid. One of Nutz's cousins was by our car . . . eating my peanut butter road snacks! He must have gotten in the car window!

Oh no! How many did you eat?
Oh, hiya, Bud. Didn't see you there.
I'm Macademia, but everyone calls me Mac.

Then Mac
tossed me a
diner takeout
menu.

We're only two stops in, Diary. I've met two of Nutz's wacky cousins. There can't be a cousin waiting for me at every stop . . . can there?

Chapter 5

ROAD TRIP WONDERS

THURSDAY

Dear Diary,

Bella woke me up bright and early today. It was a long drive to reach our third stop.

We pulled up to a log cabin.

We went inside. I was ready to snuggle down for a snooze.

So soft.
So squishy.

But Bella had other plans . . .

Come on, Bub!
Stop number three awaits.
The biggest lake in the country!

Biggest LAKE????

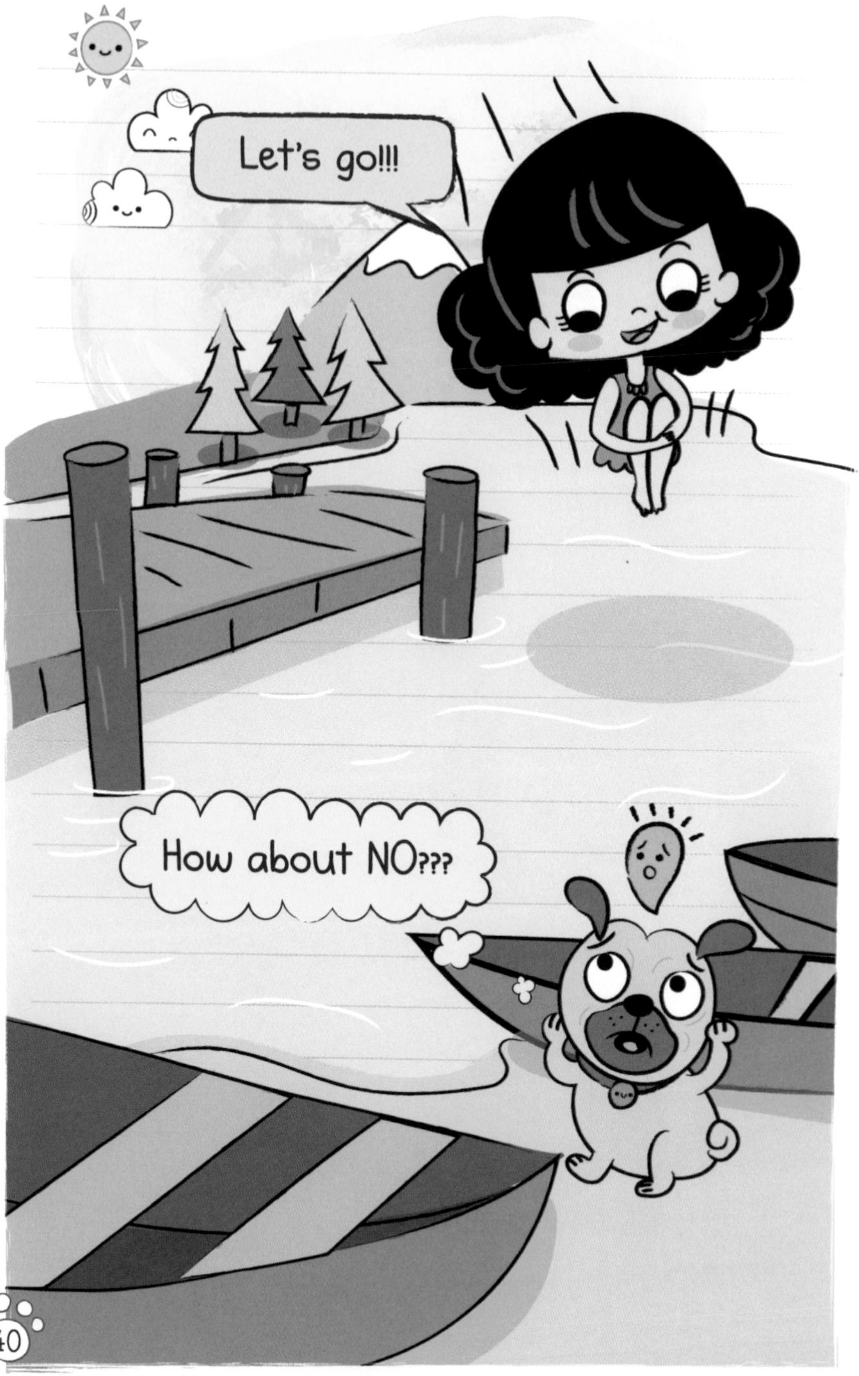
Let's go!!!
How about NO???

Luckily, Bella saw something that distracted her from the lake.

Look, Bub! A forest tour is about to start. We should go! It will be like a bonus stop!

NEXT FOREST TOUR IN 15 MINUTES. YOU'VE NEVER SEEN TREES THIS BIG!

The forest ranger told us the trees were hundreds of years old. And they were hundreds of feet tall!

Now, large trees mean lots of critters. So, please don't feed the wildlife.

Look how big they are, Bub!

I'm glad our tree fort isn't up that high.

DON'T FEED THE SQUIRRELS

I'm going to grab Jack two souvenirs from that stand—one for the lake and one for these trees!

Okay. I'll have a snack while I wait.

Diary, have you ever gotten the feeling someone is watching you?

HEY, BUZZ, MY NAME'S WALT. IT'S SHORT FOR WALNUT.

ACK!!

I picked up my treats as fast as I could, but Walt still got some.

I only have a few road snacks left, Diary. I can't afford to lose any more!

Bella says our last stop is the BIGGEST one of all. She promised there won't be any water there. I just hope there won't be any squirrels, either.

Chapter 6

END OF THE ROAD

FRIDAY

Dear Diary,

Today was the day. The last stop of Bella and Bub's BIG Road Trip! I saw fewer and fewer trees and more and more desert.

No lakes in sight!

Bella and Bub's BIG Road Trip

We drove until the road ended.

Bella said this was our last chance to get Jack a souvenir. There weren't any gift shops here. But she had a plan.

Bella dug through her backpack for her camera. Her bag was full of Jack's souvenirs.

Meanwhile, I wanted just one more snack. There wasn't a squirrel in sight. And a moment this special deserved a special treat, right?

Then I heard a sound.

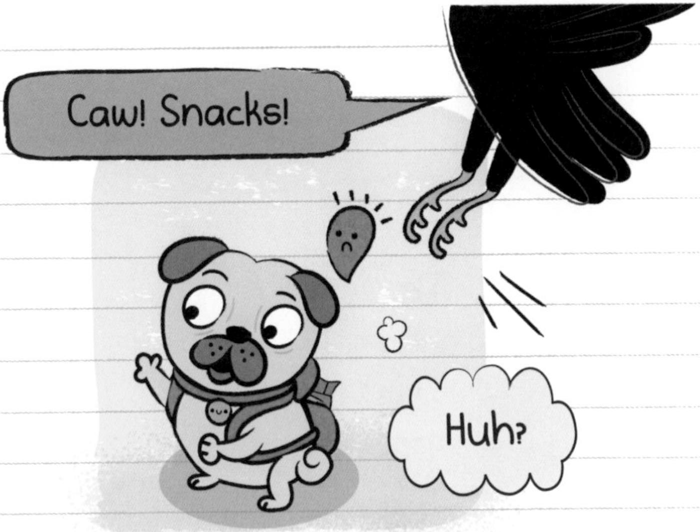
Caw! Snacks!
Huh?

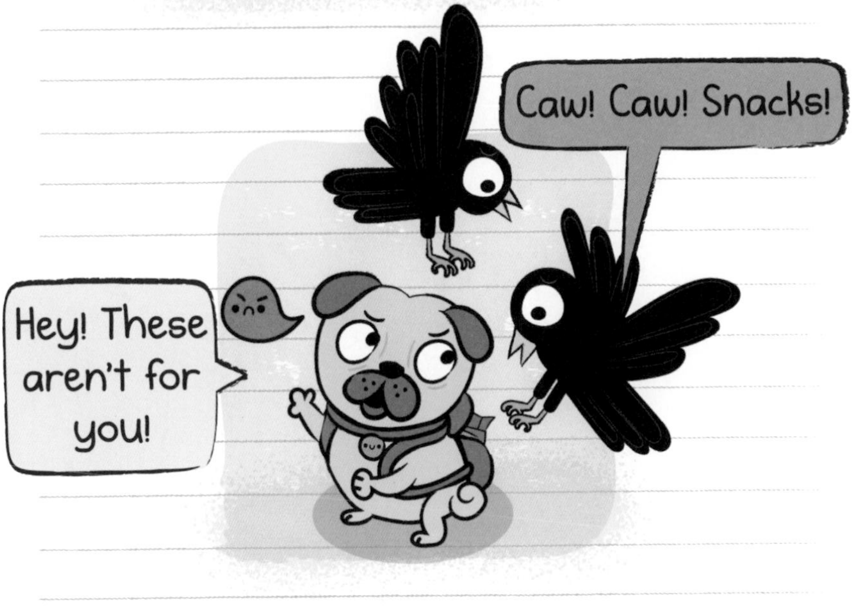
Caw! Caw! Snacks!
Hey! These aren't for you!

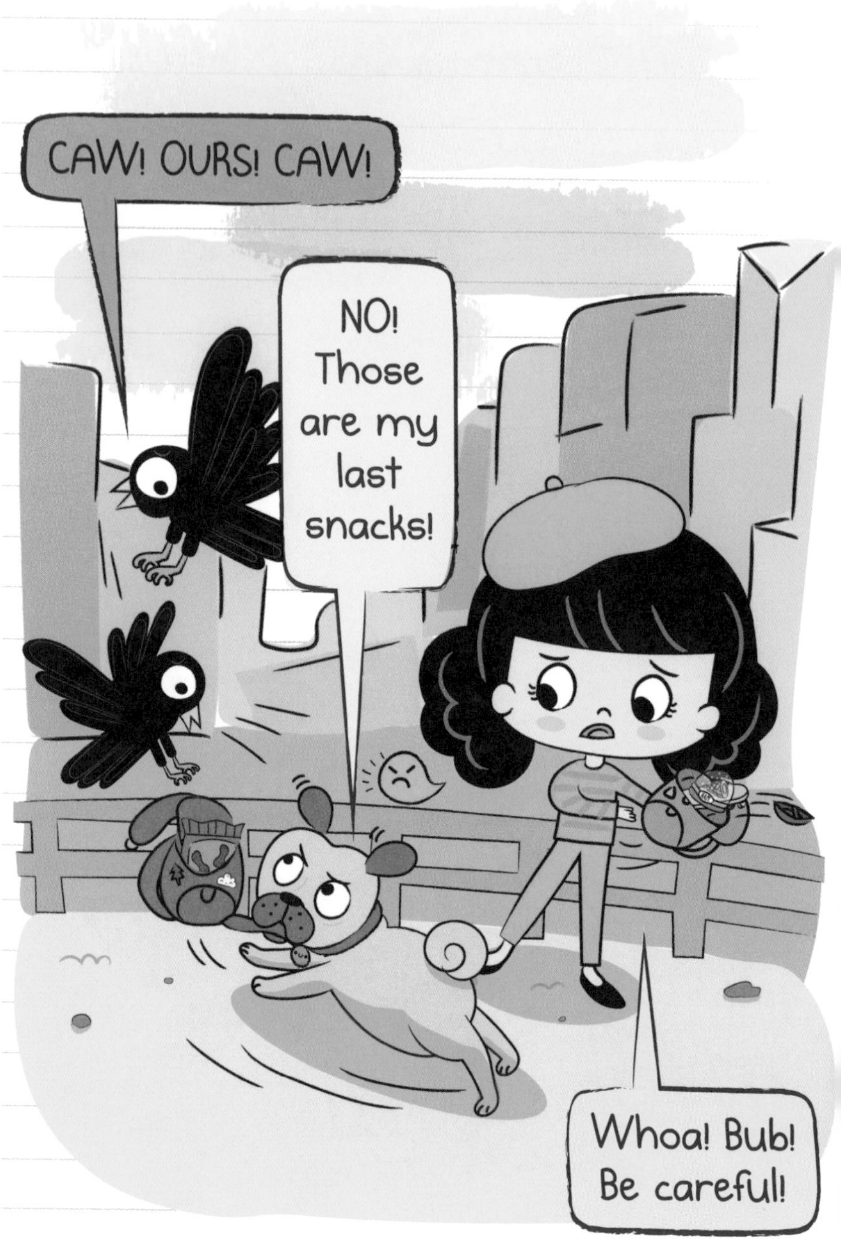
CAW! OURS! CAW!
NO! Those are my last snacks!
Whoa! Bub! Be careful!

Diary, those crows were strong. When I finally pulled my backpack away from them, I crashed into Bella—and she dropped her backpack!

No! My backpack! The souvenirs!

Bella's mom got the canyon ranger.

These crows sure are bold!

Best to keep those snacks in your bag.

The ranger helped us find Bella's backpack on the trail below.

Oh no!
Everything
is broken!

I felt terrible, Diary. Now we had nothing to bring home for Jack, and it was all my fault. What were we going to do?

Chapter 7

BUMP IN THE ROAD

SATURDAY

Dear Diary,

We started the long drive home this morning. Bella was still sad. I wished I could fix things. But short of taking the whole road trip again, what could we do?

Even the sky seems sad.

I tried to cheer Bella up with a snuggle.

Aw, Bubby. I just feel terrible that we let Jack down.

But it's not our fault. Those crows ruined everything!

Maybe a treat would make her feel happy instead.

I was digging out the last of my snacks when we hit a bump in the road.

Everything went flying! All those strange gifts Nutz's cousins gave me: the wheel, the menu, and the pinecone. One of the crows' feathers was there, too.

Bella's road trip map was on the car floor. Everything fell on top of it.

What's all this, Bubby? Were you collecting your own souvenirs?

Um . . . not exactly.

Then something unexpected happened. Bella looked at the gifts from Nutz's cousins. She placed her pieces of broken souvenirs next to them.

Huh. My souvenirs from the gift shops are broken. But when we put them together with your souvenirs on this map . . .

Bella smiled.

Bub! That gives me an idea for a present for Jack! It might not be the souvenirs we'd planned on. But I think it will be even better!

Bella told me her idea, Diary. It was amazing! It will take some work when we get home, but I can't wait. Who would have thought? Running into Nutz's cousins might have been a good thing after all.

Chapter 8

A ROAD TRIP TO REMEMBER

SUNDAY

Dear Diary,

Here's the thing about road trips: Coming home feels longer than getting there.

Legs . . . so stiff . . .

Welcome back, Bubbykins. Looks like you found your way home after all.

We got started on Jack's surprise right away.

We painted and painted. Then Bella took the broken souvenirs and glued them to her masterpiece.

We hung the surprise in the tree fort just as Jack came home from the doctor.

He's here! Are you ready, Bubby?

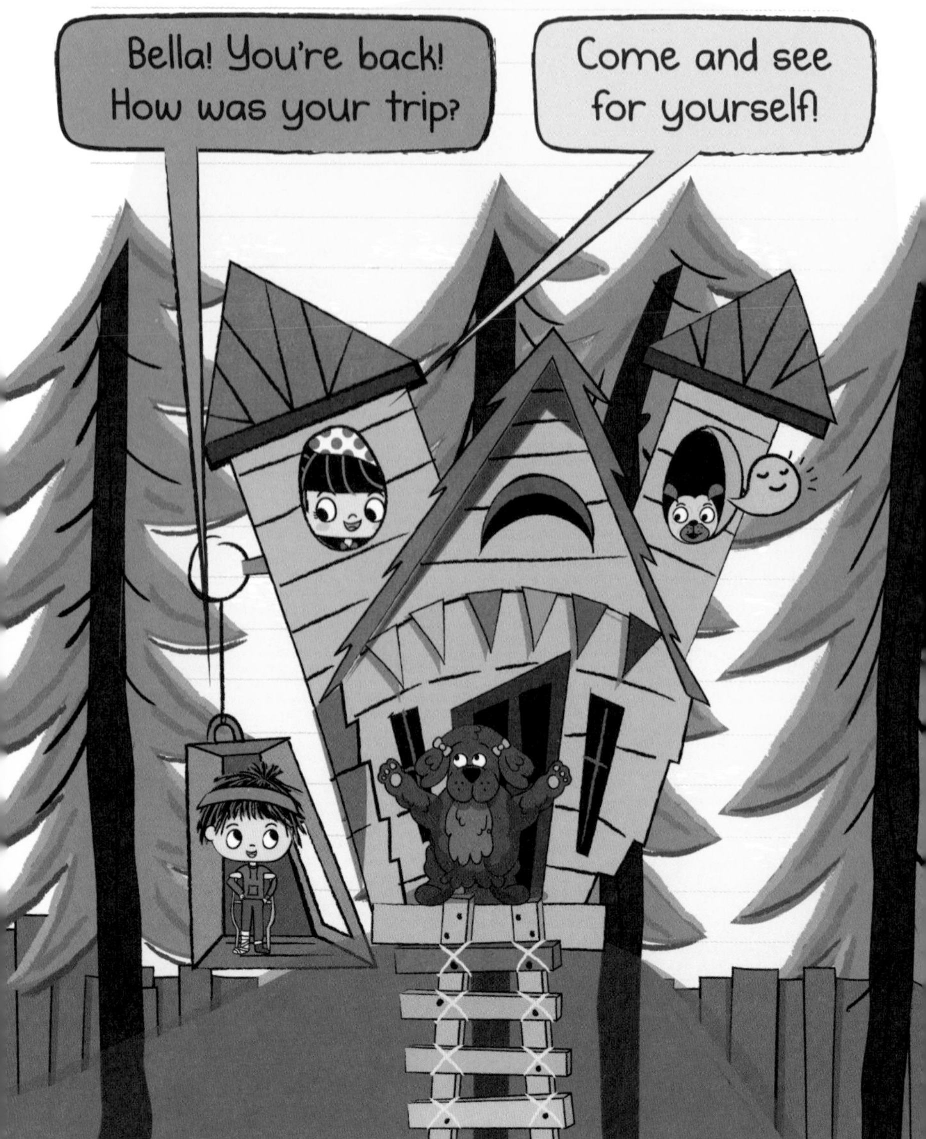
Bella! You're back! How was your trip?
Come and see for yourself!

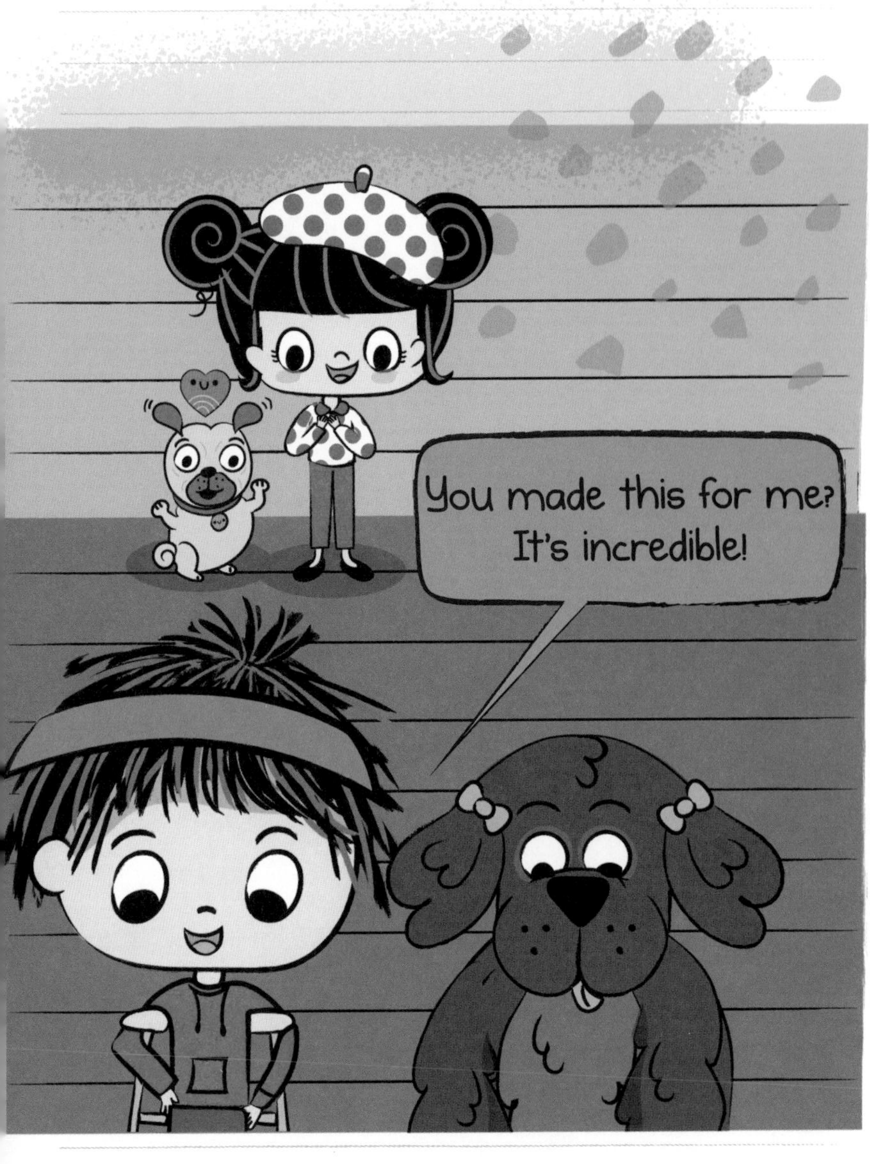
You made this for me? It's incredible!

We made Jack a one-of-a-kind, BIG road trip map from the broken souvenirs!

LAKE Awesome for doing cannonballs!

FOREST
Trees are hundreds of years old and hundreds of feet tall!

CANYON
Watch out for canyon crows!

The best big road trip is one with best friends to come home to. ♥

Jack LOVED his surprise, Diary!

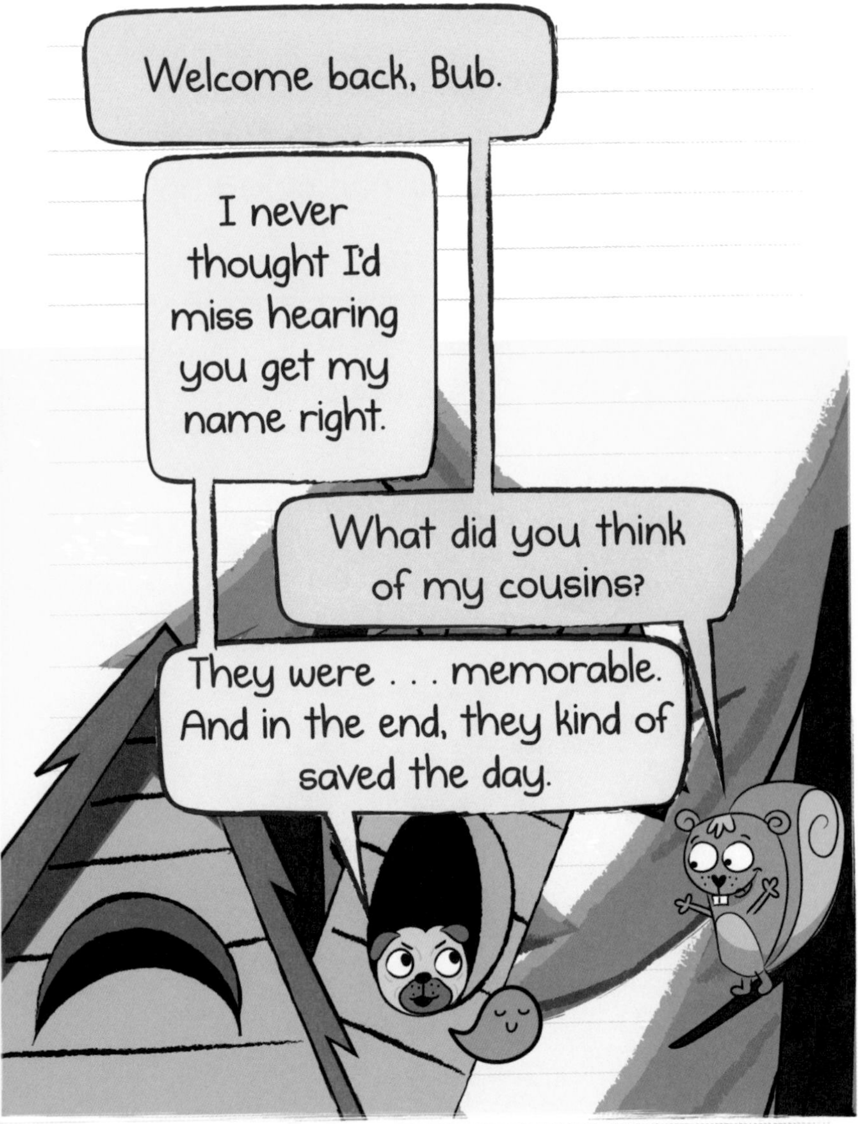
Welcome back, Bub.
I never thought I'd miss hearing you get my name right.
What did you think of my cousins?
They were . . . memorable. And in the end, they kind of saved the day.

After we gave Jack his present, I thought we were done with surprises. But it turns out Bella had picked up an extra souvenir.

Hey, Bub. I have one more surprise.

Wait! That wrapper! It couldn't be . . .

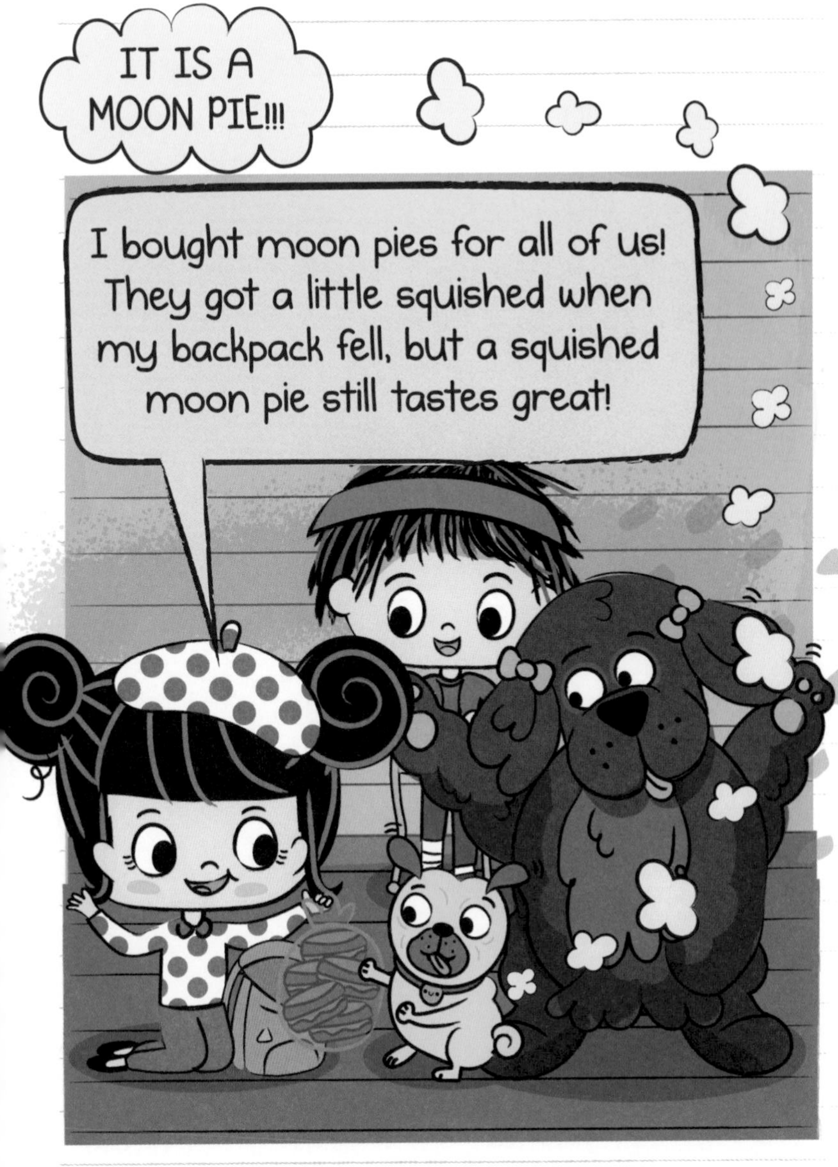
IT IS A MOON PIE!!!
I bought moon pies for all of us! They got a little squished when my backpack fell, but a squished moon pie still tastes great!

What can I say, Diary? There may have been some bumps along the way. But with memories as sweet as these, I'd call our big road trip a BIG success.

Kyla May

Kyla May is an Australian illustrator, writer, and designer. In addition to books, Kyla creates animation. She lives by the beach in Victoria, Australia, with her three daughters and two dogs. The character of Bub was inspired by her daughter's pug called Bear.

HOW MUCH DO YOU KNOW ABOUT
DIARY OF A PUG

Pug's Road Trip?

 What do I tell Bub that makes him nervous about the trip? Reread page 17.

 The names of the diner's specials include synonyms for "big" (see pages 30–31). Synonyms are words that mean the same thing. Can you spot all three synonyms for "big"?

 What gives me the idea to make a collage for Jack? Reread pages 58–60.

 Hazel, Walt, and I each give Bub a gift that seems strange at first, but turns out to be useful. Have you ever found a new way to use something?

 If you were planning a road trip, where would you go? Draw a map with all your stops.